BORIS
ON THE MOVE

by Andrew Joyner

BRANCHES

SCHOLASTIC INC.

ADVENTURES ARE ALWAYS JUST AROUND THE CORNER WITH BORIS!

Table of Contents

No part of this publication may be reproduced, stored in a retrieval system, or transmitted in any form or by any means, electronic, mechanical, photocopying, recording, or otherwise, without written permission of the publisher. For information regarding permission, write to Puffin Books, a division of Penguin Group (Australia), 250 Camberwell Road, Camberwell, Victoria 3124, Australia.

Library of Congress Cataloging-In-Publication Data

Joyner, Andrew.
Boris on the move / Andrew Joyner.
p. cm. – (Boris ; 1)
Originally published: Camberwell, Victoria, Australia : Puffin, c2011.
Summary: Boris lives in Hogg Bay, in an old bus that used to travel all over the world, but now just sits there—until one day when his parents take him on an adventure.
ISBN 978-0-545-48443-5 — ISBN 978-0-545-48442-8
1. Warthog–Juvenile fiction. 2. Natural areas–Juvenile fiction. 3. Parks–Juvenile fiction.
[1. Warthog–Fiction. 2. Natural areas–Fiction. 3. Parks–Fiction.] I. Title.
PZ7.J8573Bor 2013
823.92–dc23
2012034254

ISBN 978-0-545-48442-8 (hardcover) / ISBN 978-0-545-48443-5 (paperback)

12 11 10 9 8 7 6 5 4 3 2 1   13 14 15 16 17 18/0

Printed in China   38
First Scholastic printing, May 2013

Meet Boris.
He's a lot like you.

favorite skink

favorite drawing

favorite shorts

favorite sweater

favorite book (this week)

favorite sport

CAPTAIN CLIVE

He lives with his mom and dad.

This is Mom.

This is Dad.

He goes to school.

This is his teacher, Mrs. Huff.

This is his class.

He likes to spend time with his friends.

This is Alice.

This is Frederick.

And he likes to dream.

Boris dreams of big pets.

He dreams of big wins.

And big trips.

But mostly he dreams
about big adventures!

You'll never be bored when Boris is around!
So hitch a ride for his next adventure.

He could take you anywhere . . .
the Amazon jungle,
outer space, or maybe
just around the corner.

CHAPTER ONE

Boris lived in Hogg Bay.

He lived with his
mom and dad in an old bus.

The bus used to go everywhere.

On the road

Paris

Mexico

China

Hogg Bay

13

But that was long ago.

Now it never left the yard.

Boris wished the bus
would travel again.

Every night, Boris looked at
the map on his bedroom wall.

He'd stuck little pins all over it.

Red ones for places
he wanted to visit.

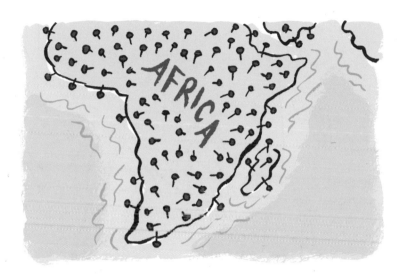

And green ones for places he had.

CHAPTER TWO

One day, Boris was reading his
favorite book. Captain Clive was
about to come face-to-face with a lion.

There was a bang!

Then a rumble and splutter.

A cloud of smoke appeared
through the back window.

The bus did something Boris
had never felt it do before.

It started to move!

It was heading out of the gate
and down the road.

All aboard!

Where are we going?

Boris ran to the back of the bus.

The bus climbed up the road
heading out of Hogg Bay.

The hill was steep.
The bus lurched and wobbled
as Mom changed gears.

CHAPTER THREE

Soon Boris couldn't see
Hogg Bay anymore.

He thought about the journey ahead.

Then the bus did something strange.

It slowed
down,

turned off
the road,

and stopped.

39

CHAPTER FOUR

Africa would take days. Weeks.

They found a picnic spot and
set up their table and chairs.

They played some games.

They found some unusual
leaves and stones.

They ate some lunch.

After lunch, Mom had an idea.

So they packed up their things
and set off down the path.

What an adventure
we're having!

CHAPTER FIVE

47

But Boris didn't look up.

He just kept walking.

And walking.

And walking.

Until he was finally having fun.

I'm Captain Clive
in the African jungle!

He clambered. He climbed.

He explored.

Then he stopped.

Boris was lost.

CHAPTER SIX

He tried to find his way back.

But it was hopeless.

Then something moved in the bushes.

It was coming closer.
Leaves rustled. Twigs snapped.

Boris almost felt scared.

But then he thought of Captain Clive.

How he had come across a lion.

He had made himself
look big and fierce.

And the lion had run away.

So Boris spread his arms out wide.

He tried to roar, but his voice
sounded funny.

Something jumped
out of the bushes.

It was coming straight for Boris. . . .

CHAPTER SEVEN

Boris opened his eyes.

There was a ginger-colored cat.

It seemed very happy
to have found Boris.

There was
another rustle
in the bushes.

BORIS!

It was Mom and Dad!
They'd found him, too!

They followed the path
back to the bus.

Mom had left a trail
of unusual stones.

Boris carried the cat all the way.

Boris thought about it
all the way home.

THE END

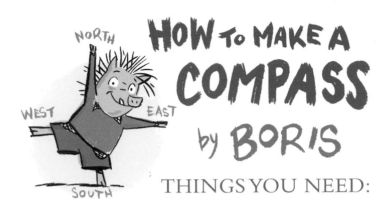

HOW TO MAKE A COMPASS by BORIS

NORTH

WEST EAST

SOUTH

THINGS YOU NEED:

1. A magnet

2. A sewing needle

3. Something small that floats, like a piece of cork or a plastic milk top— or a leaf!

4. A cup or a bowl of water

STEP 1: Turn your needle into a magnet! Rub the magnet along the needle from the eye of the needle to its point.

Now turn the page....

STEP 2: Repeat step 1 about forty times! Rub, rub, rub! *IMPORTANT: Always rub the needle in the same direction.*

STEP 3: Place your leaf (or floating thing) on top of the water so that it floats in the middle.

STEP 4: Carefully put your needle on top of the leaf. The needle will slowly turn and point NORTH. *NOW YOU'VE MADE A COMPASS!*

HOW IT WORKS: Earth is like a giant magnet. The needle of your compass is attracted to Earth's *NORTH POLE.*

NORTH

NORTH POLE

You'll never be bored when **BORIS** is around! Look for his next exciting adventure:

Boris loves pets! And he already has lots of them. All he's missing is a Komodo dragon—the biggest lizard in the world!

When Boris pretends that he's getting one, everyone in his class wants to see it. He needs to come up with a plan . . . fast! Luckily, he's got friends by his side and a trick up his sleeve!

ANDREW JOYNER has never been to Africa
or the Amazon jungle. In fact, like Boris,
he sometimes thinks, "I never go anywhere!"
He's always at home, drawing pictures and
writing stories. But then he'll step outside—
to visit his chickens or chat with his two pet
sheep—and he'll soon remember, you don't
need to travel far to find a story.